THE
DARK
CLONE

Other Scholastic books by Carol Matas:

THE DARK CLONE

Carol Matas

Cover art by Ginette Beaulieu

Scholastic Canada Ltd.
Toronto New York London Auckland Sydney
Mexico City New Delhi Hong Kong Buenos Aires

Scholastic Canada Ltd.
175 Hillmount Road, Markham, Ontario L6C 1Z7, Canada

Scholastic Inc.
555 Broadway, New York, NY 10012, USA

Scholastic Australia Pty Limited
PO Box 579, Gosford, NSW 2250, Australia

Scholastic New Zealand Limited
Private Bag 94407, Greenmount, Auckland, New Zealand

Scholastic Ltd.
Villiers House, Clarendon Avenue, Leamington Spa,
Warwickshire CV32 5PR, UK

**Library and Archives Canada Cataloguing in
Publication**

Matas, Carol, 1949-
        The dark clone / Carol Matas.
ISBN 0-439-96099-1
        I. Title.
PS8576.A7994D37 2005   jC813'.54   C2004-905884-3

6 5 4 3 2 1   Printed in Canada   05 06 07 08

*For my nephews
Michael, Mark and Jesse,
my best readers — each one a
wonderful and talented young man;
and especially for my nephew Eli,
because he loves this series
and has encouraged me to keep
telling tales about Miranda.*

Chapter 1

"Will Miranda Martin please come to the office?"

I look up in surprise. Me? I'm never called to the office. I'm never in trouble. I'm little Miss Perfect. In more ways than one.

"Miranda?" Mr. Edgers prompts me. "Are you going?"

I look at Emma. She shrugs, like, Don't look at me, I have no clue.

Slowly I gather my books, grab my knapsack and head for the door. I can't imagine what they might want me for. Maybe someone's hurt — like Ariel. That gets me moving, and I reach the office in a minute. The secretary nods when she sees me and motions me toward Mrs. Dean's office. The principal. That can't be good. I peek in the door.

Mrs. Dean notices me and waves her arm, calling me into the room and then pointing me into a seat.

"Is Ariel okay?" I ask, not able to wait for her to speak. I am clutching my knapsack as if it'll keep her from saying something I don't want to hear.

"Ariel is fine," she replies.

"My parents?"

"As far as I know, they're fine."

I am at a loss.

Mrs. Dean clears her throat. "Miranda," she says.

"Yes?"

"I really never thought I would need to have a conversation like this with you." She waits.

"Like what?" I ask.

"Come with me," she says and suddenly gets up. This is getting stranger and stranger. "Just leave your gear here."

I put my books and knapsack on the floor and follow her down the hallway — silent except for the sound of her high heels clicking on the floor. We get to the end of the hall at the back of the school and she opens the door to the outside. I am now completely mystified. She walks a short way down the path then turns back toward the building. Sprayed on the yellow stucco is large red writing: *Desert High Sucks!*

"Not very original," I comment.

"No," she agrees.

"I don't know who did it," I offer, "if that's what this is about."

"That's not what this is about, Miranda. We know who did it."

I stare at her. Why on earth involve me? I wonder.

"See the camera there?" She points up to a spot on the building where a small camera is located.

"So whoever did it is stupid, as well as un-original," I say.

"Miranda, please stop this."

"Stop what?"

She puts her hands on her hips. "We know it was you. We have the tape."

"*What?*"

"You heard me, Miranda."

"That's impossible! I didn't do it! Why would I?"

"I don't know why," she says, staring even-ly at me. "You had to realize you'd be caught.

You certainly aren't stupid."

"But I didn't!" I repeat. "How could you think for one minute I would ever do such a thing?" I pause, at a loss for words. "It's so, so . . . *childish!*"

"We can certainly agree on that," Mrs. Dean says. She pauses for a moment and then says, "Miranda, if you have a problem you can tell me. Often these incidents are a simple cry for help. I know it must be hard for you — having your cousin come to live with your family."

"Well, that's true," I agree. "Ariel can be pretty annoying. But I'm okay. I even kinda am sorta fond of her now."

Mrs. Dean raises her eyebrows.

"Well, just because I don't express myself well while talking about her doesn't mean I don't like her. I do."

"You can't deny the evidence of the tape."

"May I see it, please?" I ask.

"Of course."

We take the same silent trip back to the office. I stand as Mrs. Dean puts in the tape, then plays it. The girl looks like me, all right. Almost exactly. She is spraying the wall, quickly, efficiently, seemingly with no nervousness at all. My heart sinks. "When was this taken?"

"This morning, around six o'clock."

"I was home, in bed."

"Can anyone vouch for you?"

"No, they were asleep."

"Miranda, it couldn't be anyone but you." She pauses. "Or Ariel."

Ariel has sprouted up over the summer. When she first came to live with us it was obvious she was younger than me. And it's still obvious because she hasn't developed any, shall we say, curves. She looks like she's eleven. But the girl in the video is wearing a loose sweatshirt and an Angels baseball cap on her head, hair tucked into it. Ariel had her hair cut over the summer, and she wears it in a really cute bob, unlike mine, which is long and straight. But what with the hat it's impossible to tell anything that way. Still, to me, whoever that is looks like Ariel in age, like me in appearance. So what could that mean?

My mind starts racing, searching for an answer. Those clothes? I don't recognize them. It couldn't be Ariel. I'd know if she were up to something — wouldn't I? But if not me, or Ariel . . . Eve? But Eve is with Dr. Mullen . . .

I realize I need to say something to Mrs. D. "Mrs. Dean, I'll pay for you to get it fixed."

"Thank you, Miranda. Of course, your parents will be called."

"Of course."

"And I want you to see the school counsellor. I've made an appointment for one o'clock today. Don't miss it."

"I won't."

She waits.

"You aren't ill again, are you?" she asks.

I immediately think back to the illness that almost killed me — and would have, without Ariel's sacrifice. Unconsciously I touch the place where the scar still remains from my liver transplant. But what if there *is* something else wrong with me now — like something wrong with my brain?

I gulp and answer, "Not as far as I know." *Could* I have done it without realizing? Surely not! I woke up as usual in my bed only a few hours ago. Unless . . . now my head starts to spin. Unless I did it and managed to then get myself back home. Or maybe it *was* Ariel . . . I realize that Mrs. D. is staring at me and that, again, I need to say *something*.

"I'll do everything you say," I answer weakly.

"Fine. Go back to your class."

The lunch bell rings just as I reach class. I almost bump into Emma rushing out the door, no doubt coming to find me.

"So?" she asks.

"You won't believe it. Come with me, we need to talk."

We throw our books into our lockers, grab the brown bags we both brought today and head outside. When it's 115 degrees, not too many kids sit outside, so we have the table at the back of the school to ourselves. We can see the graffiti from where we sit.

"Not too original," Emma comments.

"Exactly what I told Mrs. Dean."

"Mrs. Dean showed it to you?"

"That's not all she showed me. She played me a tape of me doing it."

"*What?*"

"Exactly my reaction." I grimace. "Sometimes I wonder if it's you that's my clone, not Ariel."

"But Miranda, what does that mean?"

"A variety of not especially attractive

answers come to mind," I reply.

"Let's list them," Emma says, ever practical, as she takes a swig of water from her bottle. Only a minute out in the sun and we can both feel all the water from our bodies evaporating.

"Fine," I say with a sigh. "Option one: It was me and I was under some kind of spell."

"Or you are sick and don't know what you are doing," Emma says quietly, not looking at me.

"But I have no other symptoms — no headaches, no blurry vision, nothing. I feel totally normal."

"Well, that's something," Emma says. "So I doubt it's that. Let's move on. Option two?" Neither of us wanted to dwell long on option one.

"Option two: It was Ariel and she is either sick or gone crazy."

"Don't like that one," Emma grimaces.

"Option three," I continue. "It's Eve."

We both fall silent for a moment thinking about Eve. I managed to rescue Ariel and bring her to live with me, but Eve, our third clone . . . I couldn't save her.

"That's pretty unlikely," Emma says finally, "since Dr. Mullen has taken her away, and the chances of her escaping from him are close to nil. And why would she want to? He might be the only hope to cure her brain tumour! I mean, when she called you last she said Dr. Mullen had done something to help her and that she was getter better, right?"

"Which brings us to option four," I say. "There's a fourth clone."

"But surely we would have found out about a fourth clone by now?" Emma objects.

"Why?" I counter. "Mullen could have hidden one somewhere and as she was growing up kept her a secret. Now she's either escaped from him or is doing his bidding."

"And his bidding is what?" asks Emma. "To write graffiti on the school walls?"

"It does sound kind of stupid," I say. "But I did get in trouble. And maybe that's the motive."

"But why would anyone want to get you in trouble?" Emma demands.

This stymies both of us so we resort to the next logical thing to do. Eat. Maybe it'll stimulate our brains.

Emma and I gave up on school lunches ages ago and now always bring our own.

Lorna has made me roast turkey with cranberry sauce on whole grain bread. This is one of my all-time favourite sandwiches, but today I can hardly taste it. I gulp my water. "Maybe Dr. Mullen is still mad at me for rescuing Ariel."

"That could be it," Emma agrees. "Remember, he did want Ariel for his disgusting scheme."

"Oh, I remember," I say. "Using her perfect DNA to make perfect babies, so he could sell them to the highest bidder. Who could forget?"

"So we agree it's *likely* this is happening in order to get you in trouble," Emma reiterates, as she munches on her sandwich.

"Yes."

"And getting you in trouble means your reputation is damaged, even though we don't know why he would want that."

"Maybe he's planning something."

"Maybe," Emma agrees. "What worries me is what else he might do."

"I hadn't thought of that," I say. "You think I'm in for more trouble?"

Emma looks at me. "What do you think?"

"I think I'm in for more trouble," I sigh.

"Come on," says Emma, "let's get inside."

"We need to find Ariel," I say.

"Plus, there's no use having our brains fried, just when we need them," Emma grins.

I try to smile back. But it isn't easy. Something inside me just wants to stay out here in the heat and the unrelenting sun, because it's quiet and peaceful and I have a very, very bad feeling. Whoever has done this doesn't have my best interests at heart, that's for sure. Slowly I follow Emma into the cool hall. The door slams behind us with a huge bang and involuntarily I jump.

Chapter 2

We have two counsellors at Desert High, Mrs. Sanchez and Mr. Bell. The general agreement at school is that the former is cool, the latter is a goof. Naturally I get stuck with Mr. Bell. We call him Mr. Saved-by-the-Bell. He always has this crazy smile plastered on his face. "Oh, you're getting bad grades? Laugh it up! Kids are picking on you? Let a smile be your guide!"

I suppress a sigh. What on earth am I going to tell him? Let's see: Mr. Bell, I'm a clone of my dead sister Jessica, created by the mad scientist Dr. Mullen. My so-called cousin, Ariel, who just came to live with me, is a clone of me. I discovered her at Dr. Mullen's lab when he was treating me for a rare illness. It turns out that my parents had her created as an insurance policy, in case I ever needed spare parts, but I wouldn't let them murder her for that. Instead she gave me half her liver, which cured me just fine, thank you, and then she came to live with me. She's four years younger than I am so she doesn't look exactly like me, but she will. And oh, yes, there's a third clone, Eve, who has a deadly brain tumour, who at first pretended to be Ariel and fooled me, and swapped herself for Ariel when Dr. Mullen wanted Ariel back and tricked him, too, and also made him pretty mad. And now there's a fourth clone, we think, and it doesn't look good for me right now.

Yeah, they'd lock me up in a second.

"Miranda?" Mr. Bell is looking at me curiously. "Miranda, you're talking to yourself."

"Did I say anything out loud?" I ask, horrified.

"Something about things not looking too good for you."

"Oh," I say, relieved. "Well, that's true. They don't."

"I understand you refuse to admit you've done this, even though we have the proof on tape?"

"Maybe I'm sleepwalking?" I suggest, grasping at straws. "I've heard that crazy things can happen when you sleepwalk."

Mr. Bell brightens. "That's true! Why, that's a perfectly logical explanation." I can't believe he's falling for it.

But his brows knit together. "Still, what we need to figure out, Miranda, is why your subconscious would make such a statement. You have a 4.0 average. You dance brilliantly, and you're a promising actress. Everything you do, you do well. Perhaps you are putting too much pressure on yourself to be perfect?"

"But I have to be perfect," I say.

"Why?" he asks.

"I'm just made that way, I guess," I answer.

"Miranda, I must disagree," Mr. Bell counters. "We can choose who we are."

"Do you really believe that?"

"Of course I do! Otherwise I'd be out of business, wouldn't I?"

"Do you choose to be Mr. Smiley Face all the time?" I blurt out.

The grin fades from his face for a moment and then returns stronger than ever. "Touché," he declares. "But yes, I do. Okay, I'll admit I'm naturally cheerful. But I could easily make myself miserable, I'm sure."

"No, you couldn't," I object. "See, I upset you for a second, but your fall-back position is to be happy. Mine is to be perfect!"

"Let's say for a moment that's true," he concedes. "I have read studies which suggest we all have a certain set point. People who win lotteries go back to being the way they were about a year after their win. People who have bad luck — become paralyzed, for instance — also go back to their set point, happy or depressed, a year or so after the terrible event. But perhaps part of you doesn't *want* to be perfect anymore."

Wrong, I think, part of whoever that clone is doesn't want me to be perfect anymore.

"Or," he suggests, "are your parents pressuring you to do well?"

"No," I sigh, "they think I'm perfect no matter what I do."

"That's both good and bad," he says. "You might feel you always have to live up to that."

I need to wrap this up. After all, I can't really level with him.

"Maybe you're right," I agree. "So what do I do?"

"Just cut yourself some slack," he advises.

"That's it?"

"That's it."

"So, can I go?"

"Sure. But you'll need to check in with me twice a week for the next month or so. Agreed?"

"Agreed," I say.

Well, that wasn't so bad, I think as I walk back to class.

The PA system crackles: *"Will Miranda Martin please come to the office?"*

I stop dead. My heart sinks. Now what?

I turn slowly and head over to the office. Classes are changing, the halls are full. Everyone is looking at me. A few kids shout at me. "In trouble again? Oooh, Miranda, bad girl!"

Bad girl? Wow, never thought I'd hear that said about me. I get to the office. Two police officers are in the outer office talking to Mrs. Dean.

"Please," she says to them as I come in. "In my office." She shows them the way. I follow, heart in my throat.

"Miranda Martin?" The police officer is a young woman. Her partner is an older man.

"Yes?"

"We have evidence that you have been shoplifting at SuperMart."

I stare at her. "I've never shopped at SuperMart in my life."

"I didn't say shop," she says sternly. "I said shop*lifting*."

"It wasn't me," I say, but I know it's in vain. They'll have it on tape.

"We have you on tape. We showed a photo from the security camera to your principal, who identified you. It wasn't too bright of you to wear a Desert High sweatshirt, led us right here to the school."

"When did this supposedly happen?" I ask.

"Yesterday afternoon at five o'clock."

"I was at home with my cousin," I say.

"How old is your cousin?"

"She's eleven."

"Were there any adults present?"

"No."

"Well," she says, "we'd better speak to your cousin."

Mrs. D. pushes the intercom on her desk and asks Ariel to come to the office. We all stand around awkwardly while we wait for her to arrive. When she comes in looking happy, curious, and so innocent, I get a rush of feeling for her and want to dash over and give her a big hug. I don't, though.

"Ariel," Mrs. D. says, "what did you do yesterday?"

"I was at school," she answers with certainty. "And after that I hung out with Miranda," she adds rather proudly.

She loves to hang out with me, but I'm usually busy with Emma or my other friends and I encourage her to hang with her own friends. Still, her favourite thing is for the two of us to swim in the pool or go shopping. Yesterday, even though it was way too hot, I agreed to a swim.

"Where were your parents?" Mrs. D. asks.

"I am unsure," she answers, "but they were not at home."

The policewoman hesitates for a moment. Ariel certainly seems to be telling the truth, and I'm sure the policewoman is experienced at picking up on whether people are lying or not. "Thank you, Ariel. You can go back to class."

Ariel leaves, and the policewoman turns to me. "This is a very serious offence. Do you understand?"

"Yes, I do. But really, I didn't do it! You can see that Ariel and I were together."

"You might have told her what to say," the woman says.

"Well, I didn't! Can I at least see this tape?"

"The store intends to press charges. You can see the tape at some point."

"I would really like to see it," I insist.

The two officers look at each other. "We can show you the photo," the woman says.

It's grainy and not a great shot. The hair is under a cap and the sweatshirt covers the body, but it looks to me like a younger version of me. If Ariel hadn't been with me I'd have said it was, in fact, her.

"Can I call my parents?"

"You may."

I use the phone and call. Mother, thank goodness, is home.

"Mother, please stay calm," I say. I quickly explain what has happened.

"It wasn't you, Miranda?"

"No, Mother."

"Of course it wasn't. You would never do such a thing. But what about Ariel? She could have done it!"

"We were together," I say, trying to stay calm and not blow up at her. Typical of her to blame Ariel.

"I'll be right there."

I hang up. "My mother is on her way."

We wait for about twenty minutes, me sitting on a chair in the outer office. Mother *and* Father arrive and Mrs. Dean shows them into her office. After a few minutes the police come out, walk past without a glance and keep going. Mrs. Dean calls me back into the office.

Father speaks first. "Miranda, I've assured Mrs. Dean that this is some kind of hoax. We've seen the photo and although we admit it looks like you, it could easily be someone made up to look like you. Mr. Gonzales, our lawyer, will be dealing with the store and I doubt they will press charges after he gets them to see reason."

Mrs. Dean looks at me with some relief. "Well, I'm sure you'll get this all straightened out," she says lamely. "Do you want to go home with your parents now?"

"Maybe that would be best," my father says, not letting me answer. "Ariel will have to come, too."

"I'll just go get my books," I say. Instead of going straight to my locker I head to chem lab and peek in at the window until Emma sees me. In a minute she's out in the hall whispering with me.

"What was it?"

"Only the police! Caught me on tape shoplifting at SuperMart."

"You? At SuperMart? That's a laugh!"

"Emma, my parents are here. They're taking me and Ariel home."

"Don't worry, Miranda," she says. "We'll figure this out." She goes back to class and I head back to the office after grabbing my knapsack and books. Ariel is already in the outer office with her stuff.

Once we're all in the car Mother starts. "Mrs. Dean told us about the graffiti as well. Now Miranda, can you assure us this isn't you?"

"Yes," I say, exasperated. "It was not me."

"And Ariel," mother says sternly. "Perhaps it is you?"

"Me?" Ariel repeats. "I fail to understand. Why would I write graffiti and steal? I would never shame Miranda in such a way."

I notice that when she gets upset she

reverts back to the formal way of speaking she learned in the lab from Dr. Mullen.

"Where are we going?" I ask, noticing Father hasn't taken the exit that leads to our ranch.

"To the clinic, of course, to see your doctor," Mother replies. "They're expecting us."

I almost object, but then when I think about it for a moment realize that I'm actually a bit relieved. At least Emma and I can rule out my being crazy because of some sort of tumour or something . . . *if* the tests are all clean.

"Ariel will be checked as well," Father adds.

As I go through all the tests — bloodwork, an MRI and a physical exam by Dr. Corne, I can't help but think about the last time we were here, getting Eve checked, and how that turned out. I can still hear his words: "She has a brain tumour." And then he went on to say it was incurable. Is that what's happening to me? Or Ariel? She's getting the works as well.

But this time the results are normal for both of us. Mother looks years younger after Dr. Corne tells us the good news. And I must admit it's a weight off my mind.

On the way home Father again turns to the problem at hand. What's going on?

"What worries me is that whoever is behind this seems intent on damaging you," Father says, as he drives.

"I know!" I agree. "That's what Emma and I think. But why?"

"Why indeed?"

"Maybe we shouldn't go away this weekend," Mother says to Father.

"I don't like to go either," he agrees. "But we need this deal." He thinks for a minute. "We'll cut it short, be sure to be back by Monday. Do you think you'll be all right?" he asks me.

"If I don't end up in jail, you mean?" Although normally I'd be glad to be rid of them, I'm a little nervous now about their leaving. I mean, who knows what else someone will try to pin on me?

"If this deal doesn't go through, we'll be ruined financially," Father says. "The buyout from our clinics was just enough to set us up to acquire this company. It's a great deal and you'll be set for life. This is important too, Miranda."

"I think I'm smart enough to make my own living," I answer sullenly.

"And you are. But," he answers slowly, as if reluctant to say it, "we don't know what kind of medical costs you and Ariel might incur."

"No," I snap, "we don't." Who knows what conditions the cloning might cause. Premature aging? Cancers? Madness?

I sigh.

"We'll get back as soon as the deal is signed," Mother assures me. "In the meantime stay close to home. All right? And Mr. Gonzales will be on call all weekend in case you need him. He won't let anyone put you in jail, no need to worry about that. In fact by the time he's finished with SuperMart they'll be wishing they never bothered with that tape."

For once I'm glad to have one of their ruthless cohorts on my side.

But I have a bad feeling. If Dr. Mullen is behind this, why stop at shoplifting? He must have other nasty surprises up his sleeve. Just how far will he go? But the bigger question is, *why?* Why is this happening?

Chapter 3

The phone rings and wakes me up. It's Saturday morning and Emma is screaming into the receiver. Something about N. *N?*

"Emma, stop!" I exclaim. "What? I can't understand you."

"CNN!" She shouts.

"What about it?"

"CNN. Turn it on!"

I grab the clicker from the floor where I tossed it last night and turn on the TV. Ariel walks in as I do and exclaims, "Dr. Mullen!"

"Shshsh!" I put a hand on her shoulder and pull her onto the bed.

Dr. Mullen is speaking.

"Yes, I repeat, I have created the first human clone."

I stop breathing. Ariel lets out something

between a gasp and a cry.

I whisper into the phone. "Has he said my name yet?"

"No, no," Emma screams back. "Not yet. Quiet."

I clutch the phone and listen. And stare. Underneath Dr. Mullen is a headline that in bold letters announces: *Clinic in Belize.*

"Belize?"

"Belize is a country situated in Central America," Ariel states.

And then a thought strikes me. I'm probably still dreaming. That's it! This is, of course, the nightmare I've feared ever since I found out that I was the first human clone. Discovery. CNN and all the rest camped out at my doorstep. School an impossibility. My friends looking at me like I'm some sort of — well, like what I am. Not quite human. Unable to protect Ariel from the media, unable to lead a normal life. I close my eyes and will myself to wake up.

"Did you hear that?"

I had tuned out. Why listen? It's all a dream anyhow.

"No," I say.

Emma is screaming into the phone again.

"It's not you!"

"What?" I say.

"Listen! Look!"

A picture fills the screen. A beautiful face. A perfect face. Black hair. Large blue eyes. A baby.

"Adam," Dr. Mullen is saying. "We call him Adam. He is the clone of a young man who died all too young. His parents saved some tissue. And this, this is the result." The camera pulls back. A nurse walks onto the stage holding a small bundle and then shows it to the camera. The crowd of reporters gasps.

"Emma," I say into the phone. "This is a dream, right?"

I know how silly a question that is, but it's okay to be silly in dreams. I would like to wake up, though.

"Miranda," Emma says, finally not screaming, "this is no dream. You are awake. I swear."

"You'd swear in a dream."

"Get Ariel to pinch you."

"What will that prove?" I say. "She could pinch me in a dream."

The call waiting beeps. I look. Mother's cell.

"That's my mother," I say.

"Is she part of the dream too?"

"Hang on." I press flash.

"Miranda?"

"Yes."

"Are you watching TV, by any chance?"

"Yes."

"Now stay calm."

"I'm calm. I'm dreaming."

"No, dear, you aren't. Unless it's the same dream the rest of the world is having."

The phone drops from my hand.

"Miranda?" I hear her voice from far away. Ariel picks up the receiver.

"Mother?"

I can't hear what they are saying. I stare at the TV.

Dr. Mullen is speaking.

"Adam is healthy and completely normal in every way."

"Mother and Father are catching the first flight home," Ariel announces. "And Emma is on her way over. It appears," she adds, "that this weekend will be slightly more interesting than we assumed."

I continue to stare at the screen.

"Quiet," I say. "We'd better hear the rest.

He could name us next."

The news conference seems to drag on forever. Ariel and I sit and watch, waiting, waiting, for Dr. Mullen to tell the world about us. But then it's over. Well, the story isn't over. CNN is now interviewing every scientist and senator they can find. But nothing about us. Nothing.

"I don't understand," I say to Ariel. "I'm the first human clone. Why is Dr. Mullen saying it's this boy?"

"Adam," Ariel says.

"Adam, poor kid," I say. "Still, I don't get it."

"Perhaps," Ariel suggests, "Adam's parents want the world to know. Or it was part of the deal they made with Dr. Mullen."

"And we didn't want the world to know," I reply. "Plus he can't tell the world about us — he was going to murder you for your liver, and who knows how many other clones may have died. This way, he's done nothing illegal."

"Yes, that is accurate," she agrees.

Our housekeeper, Lorna, knocks and opens the door. "I thought I heard you calling."

I've never figured out how much Lorna knows. She's not stupid. She must know a lot. After all, she knew Jessica, the original me, the one who died. And she knows I'm exactly like her, and that I just appeared. And the same with Ariél. But every time I've asked her she just shrugs and says, "Your parents do what's best, Miranda."

"There's quite a news story on CNN," I say, "the first human clone. And Dr. Mullen is announcing it."

She goes pale. "They give a name?"

"Yes," I answer. "Come on, Lorna. Tell me. You know all about this, don't you?"

"I know some things," Lorna answers, reluctantly. "What name did they give?"

"Adam," Ariel interjects.

Honestly! If she'd been quiet I might have gotten Lorna to spill the beans.

"Adam? But that's a boy."

"It appears that Dr. Mullen has cloned a boy," I confirm.

"Well, well," Lorna nods. "What do you two want for breakfast?"

"Breakfast?" I exclaim in disbelief. "Who could eat?"

"*I* could," Ariel says. "Could I have a pepper omelette please, Lorna? And pancakes?"

I stare at Ariel. "You're joking, right?"

"No," Ariel replies. "I'm hungry!"

"Emma is on her way over, Lorna," I say. "Could you make enough pancakes for her?"

Lorna nods. "Emma can always eat," she says with approval. "You should be more like that."

I go to the bathroom, scrub my face and brush my teeth, then put on brown capris and a short sleeved brown and green striped shirt. Talk about being programmed — despite the catastrophe I still am picky about how I dress! When I emerge I see that Ariel has also gotten dressed. She's in jeans and her new sandals and an orange polo T-shirt and she's watching TV again.

"Dr. Fisher. Do you think this is the real thing?" The CNN anchor asks.

"We have no way to know unless they allow us to verify the entire process independently."

"I understand," says the anchor, "that a very large sum of money has already been offered to the parents for their story. And that the publishers have hired their own medical teams."

"Yes, I've heard that as well," the doctor answers. "I'd love to be part of that team."

The doorbell rings. "Emma!" I exclaim. "Thank goodness."

We both tear out to the front hall, Ariel just beating me to the door to open it. Emma waves at her brother who has dropped her off. We live just outside the city of La Quinta on a ranch — well, it's not a real ranch. Lots of cactus and landscaping and palm trees and gardens. I was hoping to get a horse this year, but what with all the money problems I'll be lucky to get anything for Christmas. Well, I guess now I'd settle for Dr. Mullen not giving my name to the media.

Chapter 4

"Is that pancakes I smell?" Emma asks.

"Yes," I say, punching her on the shoulder.

"Just because the world as we know it is coming to an end doesn't mean a person can't be hungry," Emma protests.

I follow her and Ariel to the kitchen and watch as they tuck into their breakfasts. I eat half a grapefruit, picked fresh from our yard, and a piece of toast with some marmalade. And I steal a corner of Ariel's omelette.

"Hey!" she protests.

"So now what?" I ask the two of them, ignoring Ariel's dirty look.

"I'm not sure," Emma says, waiting until Lorna is out of the room. "So far it looks like this won't affect you and Ariel. It looks like

Dr. Mullen is going to leave you out of this altogether."

"If you think we're coming out of this free and clear," I say grimly, "you've got another think coming. No good can come of this. Something is bound to go wrong. People are going to find out about us. After all, they'll be snooping into everything Dr. Mullen has ever done. Plus, we can't forget, there may even be a fourth clone. Someone is trying to get me in trouble, and it has to be connected to this announcement somehow. I feel like my head is going to explode." I turn to Emma. "What about your dad? He can tell us what to do."

"He could if he wasn't hiking with my mom in the desert," Emma says. "But they're supposed to be home tomorrow, anyway. I've paged him. If they aren't out of range, maybe they'll come home faster."

I nod. Emma's dad, Dr. Green, took over the administration of Dr. Mullen's clinic and knows the whole story. He is the only adult I can trust. My mother and father, who lied to me about who I was, *what* I was, I can never trust again. How can I, after I found out that they'd lied to me for years? How can I, when they conspired with Dr. Mullen to *murder*

Ariel — even if it was to save me?

Ariel snaps me out of my thoughts. "What do we do in the meantime?"

"Try not to let our heads explode," Emma suggests.

I slip out of the kitchen onto the patio by the pool, leaving them to finish their food. I don't understand how Emma and Ariel can be treating this all so lightly. It's a disaster of the first order. In all likelihood my life as I know it is over from this moment on. It's true that in a way, my life changed irrevocably as soon as I discovered I was a clone. But at least I could hope, could envisage, a normal life. After all, no one in the outside world would know. Now they are bound to find out, no matter how hard we try to stop them. And another, more troubling thought occurs to me. Perhaps I *will* have to come forward. If I don't, Dr. Mullen will be viewed as some sort of genius, he'll be revered, instead of shown up for what he is — an evil, horrible man, out for himself and no one else. A murderer. Someone who sees us as property to sell, not human. With enough money, enough support, how many more of us could he create? And yet, if I expose Mullen I'll expose not only myself, but Ariel and my parents. My parents could go to jail for conspiracy to murder! And then what would happen to me and Ariel? Some horrible foster home where we were viewed as freaks? Not to mention the guilt of seeing my parents suffer in jail.

I don't hear Emma and don't realize she's followed me until she sits on the wicker chair next to me.

"How are you?" she asks.

"Brain exploding as we speak," I reply.

"I know, me too," she says, sympathetically. "It has so many implications for everyone, doesn't it? Even my dad, who knew all about it but didn't turn in your parents. Even he could get in trouble, maybe lose his medical license."

"I hadn't thought of that," I say. "It just gets worse and worse."

"I know," Emma agrees, "but I don't think we should upset Ariel any more than we need to. She doesn't realize what this could mean."

"Yeah, you're right."

"So what should we do?" she asks.

I put my head in my hands. I have a strong urge to burst into tears.

We can hear the phone ringing and soon Ariel is out on the porch, phone still in hand. She puts it down on the table. "Your parents are at the airport in Frankfurt. They won't be home till tomorrow morning, though."

"Just as well," I mutter. "They'll only make things worse, no doubt."

Ariel grimaces. "Miranda, you are very hard on them. They have been trying very hard to make it up to you. They love you." She pauses. "You are fortunate."

I feel terrible. Poor Ariel. My parents accepted her into our home when I insisted, telling the world that she's my cousin. But they never really warmed to her. It's me they love; they've never accepted her as their daughter. It's ironic because she'd be willing to love them, whereas I can barely tolerate them. I know they created a clone of me for my sake, out of love, and that they cloned me from Jessica out of love, but that is no excuse. People do all sorts of horrible things in the name of love. It doesn't make it right.

Before Emma has a chance to say anything, the phone rings again. I answer.

"Miranda," a small voice says.

"Yes."

"It's Eve."

"Eve!"

I shout at Emma and Ariel. "It's Eve!"

"Is she all right?" Emma asks.

"Are you all right?" I repeat.

"So far."

"What does that mean?" I ask.

"Dr. Mullen seems to have forgotten all about me. I don't know where I am. Locked up somewhere. And he hasn't been to visit in weeks. Not even to do tests on me or anything."

"Maybe that's a good thing," I suggest.

"Perhaps," Eve replies. "He says I am cured."

"But that's wonderful," I say, giving a thumbs up to Emma and Ariel.

"Yes. Except now the headaches are back. And he's lost interest in me. And I don't know what it all means."

"Well, first thing you have to do," I say, shaking my head at Emma and Ariel, "is to find out where you are. We need to get you out of there. Who's minding you?"

"A couple of nurses."

"What are they like?"

"Bored."

"Bored," I muse. "Well, then you should be able to take advantage of any lapses they have. Or outsmart them. You're calling here. How did you manage that?"

"I lifted the phone from the living room."

I smile. "What's the area code on the number?"

"Just a minute. 760."

"760?" I repeated. "You're here! Right here in the desert. You just need to get out of there and we'll find you."

"Must go." And then, *click*, the line goes dead.

"You heard?" I ask Emma and Ariel.

"She's here?"

"And I thought Dr. Mullen would take her far away so the authorities wouldn't find him — or her," I say.

"Perhaps he did. He might have flown her back here without her knowing. Or made sure she was so drugged she couldn't remember. Is she all right?"

I tell them what she told me.

"Maybe he needed to get her out of the way before he made the announcement about Adam," Emma suggests.

"True," I agree. "A defective clone isn't good for business, is it?"

"In that case, I think we need to go find Eve," Emma says with some urgency.

"You're right. I wouldn't put anything past Mullen. Maybe he's left her to die." Then something occurs to me. "You don't think he would be keeping her at his old clinic, do you?"

"No, my dad cleaned it up, fired everyone who used to work for Mullen. He couldn't even get in."

Of course. I'm not thinking straight. I knew that.

"Wait!" I exclaim. "We can reverse dial, get the phone number and then trace it online."

I do that, then head to my room where my iMac is set up. I do a reverse directory search and within minutes I've found the house. It's in La Quinta.

"Would he stick her anywhere so obvious?" Emma asks. "It's too easy."

I pause to think about that. The worst scenario comes to mind. "Maybe it didn't matter where. He figures she'll be dead soon, and then she won't be a problem."

Ariel and Emma stare at me. I can see that

makes sense to them — too much sense, unfortunately.

"We need to find her," I continue. "If she's dying we don't want it to be with strangers."

"But how?" Ariel asks.

"Yes, how?" Emma echoes.

"It is very annoying being stuck out here," I say, stating the obvious. Although even if we were in one of the cities, we wouldn't have a car. And like everywhere in California, you pretty much need one — or a parent to drive you. "Bikes?" I suggest.

The other two nod. No choice. I'm strong enough to double up with Eve if we're lucky enough to find her. Ariel has a brand new bike. I also have a new one, and there are two pretty decent older ones my parents use. Emma takes my mom's.

I check MapQuest first, and then we set off — after Ariel has made sure we are all slathered with sunscreen. She's become some sort of health fanatic because she worries that both of us are susceptible to all kinds of diseases, especially cancer. Who knows what our genetic makeup might spring on us next?

It takes us about a half hour to get to the address in La Quinta, which turns out to be near the Polo Grounds. It's in a subdivision of large homes, a gated community with a guard. This poses a problem. How to get in?

Chapter 5

We huddle together on the grass, away from the gate so the guard doesn't see us and become suspicious. We are exhausted. I drink at least half my water and make Ariel do the same. It's only 105 degrees today, which feels almost cool compared to the 115 it's been for the last week. Still, that's still plenty hot if you're riding your bike for a half hour in the sun.

"Do you think we could come up with a story the guard would believe?" Emma asks.

"I doubt it," I reply. "They won't let you in unless you have a person to call." I look at the wall built around the complex. "It isn't too high," I remark. "We could probably climb over if we used our bikes to hike us up. Let's ride around and see if we can find a spot where no one will see us."

We get onto our bikes and drive down the nearest side street. When we reach the end, we see that the complex is part of a large golf course, with condos built around the course.

"We may be able to get in through the golf course," Emma suggests.

She's right, of course. I've always wondered why people bother with the gates and guards when you can just get in a back way. We keep riding until we finally do see an opening, a fairway that flows into a wash. We get off our bikes and walk them over the wash, hurry through the fairway — I really don't want to die being hit on the head with a golf ball — and find ourselves at the back of a cul-de-sac.

This neighbourhood is made up of large individual homes. We must be talking in the millions and up. I take the map I printed up out of my knapsack.

"We're on," I look around, "Hummingbird Drive. And the address is here," I point, "on Blackbird Way. So we go," I pause to get my bearings, "that way."

It takes us another ten minutes before we reach the street. We ride by once, casually, looking as we go, and stop a few houses down. It's a long, low bungalow, probably at least three or four bedrooms, with a two-car garage. There's no obvious life. We walk around the house checking all the windows, but no luck. They are all dark and shuttered.

"Now what do we do?" Ariel asks.

"We could just go knock on the door," I suggest. "If one of the nurses answers, we could push our way in. Maybe Eve will hear us and she'll manage to get out."

Emma shrugs. "I can't think of anything better," she says. "Let's do it."

We pedal back to the house and leave our bikes near the street, on the well-manicured grass that they've managed to keep green despite the last month of burning sun. We walk up to the door. I pause for a second to work up some courage, then bang on the door. We listen intently. Nothing. No sound at all. I bang again. Nothing.

I turn the handle with the intention of rattling it and yelling, except the handle turns easily and the door opens.

"Whoa!" I exclaim.

"That's weird," Emma says.

"Too weird," I agree. "Should we go in?"

"Of course we should," Ariel declares, as

she pushes past me. "Maybe she's sick. I wouldn't put it past Dr. Mullen to leave her here to die all alone."

"Neither would I. But let's hurry. I don't like this. It's too . . . "

"It's too B-movie," Emma finishes my sentence. We step into the foyer. It's dark and cool, a relief from the terrible heat. The foyer opens to a living room that has drapes which probably cover the sliding doors to the backyard.

"Hello?" I call out. "Hello?"

No answer. The house has that quiet feel, no one around.

"We split up," I say. "Emma, you and I will check the bedrooms. Ariel, look in the kitchen and out back. If we can't find Eve, maybe there will be evidence that she's been here."

Ariel heads off and so do we. The house is furnished in typical desert southwestern style. There is a couch and an armchair in the living room and a TV that is on, tuned to CNN, with the sound off. It looks like more on the cloning story, but I try to shut my eyes to it and concentrate on my surroundings. This feels wrong. Plus there is a strange smell in the air. I hurry and check one of the bedrooms. It has twin beds. I look in the closet. There are clothes that would fit a girl Eve's age. So maybe she is here somewhere, or was. I look in the bathroom. Three toothbrushes. There is a door off the living room, probably a den. I open it and see what looks like a complete operating theatre with two beds, machines, wires, lights in the ceiling and a funny odour. I walk into the room. Emma comes in after me.

"The two rear bedrooms are completely empty," she says.

Just then a strange tingling sensation begins in my fingers. My knees feel all wobbly and my head starts to spin. I hear Emma's voice behind me. "Miranda, I don't feel very . . . " She doesn't finish her sentence. I turn toward her. She crumples to the floor. My head is spinning and it feels like there's a hurricane in my ears, the sound of wind rushing. Ariel comes into the room. I see her as I sit down hard on the floor. I grab Ariel's hand as she nears me.

"Get Emma out of here," I say, my voice a whisper. Ariel drags Emma out and soon is back for me. She helps me up and I stagger out into the fresh air. I collapse on the grass beside Emma, gulping air.

"Miranda," Ariel is saying, "can you hear me?"

My head starts to clear, the noise in my ears subsides, and I crawl over to Emma. Her eyes are open. She stares at me for a moment, then speaks. "What the heck just happened?"

"I'd say we were set up. There was some kind of gas in there and if Ariel hadn't gone outside we all would have succumbed. Ariel, can you get us our water?"

Ariel runs to our bikes and brings back the water. I help Emma sit up. We all take deep gulps from our bottles.

"If someone is out to do us harm, I suggest we get out of here as quickly as possible," Emma says.

I agree. "Can you get up?" I ask her.

Slowly she stands, as do I. I feel like I've been hit on the head with a hammer. We walk shakily over to our bikes, get on and start off slowly. We ride out through the front gates and then head toward Palm Desert.

I'm in the lead. After about ten minutes, I notice a small strip mall on my left, down a side street. I spot an ice cream place. We turn in, park our bikes, go inside, order some Cokes and sit down in a booth.

"What just happened?" Emma pulls her hands through her black hair. It's gone all frizzy from the heat and the ride and her eyes are looking wild.

I shake my head and take a gulp of my drink.

"Do you think it was some kind of poisonous gas?" I ask.

"Must have been," she says.

"Was the place booby-trapped?" Ariel asks.

"Maybe set to go off when we opened that door," Emma replies. She stops. "If you hadn't been outside . . . " she says to Ariel.

"We would all be dead," Ariel nods. "Yes. That is obvious."

"Not so obvious," I say. "We don't know what that gas was. Perhaps it was to knock us out, not kill us."

"Why?" Ariel asks.

"Could Dr. Mullen be after you again, I wonder?" I say, looking at Ariel. "Maybe he can't cure Eve so he still wants you back. You're the perfect clone, after all."

"So he knocks us all out and takes Ariel," Emma says. "And according to that theory what happens to you and me?"

"Maybe we don't wake up," I say. "Maybe we know too much."

"Or if we survive somehow, no one believes us because you have already been caught doing crazy things."

Any my parents wouldn't fight to get Ariel back, I think, but I don't say it out loud.

"But why would Dr. Mullen need me?" Ariel objects. "He has Adam now."

"Adam is just a baby," I point out. "What if he grows up with health problems like Eve? Or like I had? He'd want some backup, some proof that he could create a perfect clone. And you are still that proof. Not to mention the disgusting baby-selling plan — nice blonde baby girls . . . "

I feel cold all over, despite my overheated body. Is this what we have in store for us? Will Mullen never leave us alone?

"Let's say Dr. Mullen figured out we'd go looking for Eve. Does that mean Eve set us up?" Emma asks.

"No!" Ariel exclaims.

"But maybe Eve was being used by Dr. Mullen to get us out to that house," I suggest.

"If all this is true, he is a very bad person,"

Ariel says softly.

"We know he wouldn't hesitate to kill us," I say. "We found that out when we tried to rescue Eve. What on earth are we going to do?"

"I think we should still try to find Eve," Ariel says. "She may know nothing of this. And she could still be in danger."

"But we're in danger too," Emma reminds her. She looks at me. "Miranda, you have to consider going public."

"Telling the world about the evil Dr. Mullen?" I say.

"Yes!" says Emma. "He *is* evil. I'm sure he's behind this. And who knows what other horrible things he's doing. He could be creating clones and killing off the ones he doesn't like, the ones that aren't good enough. We have to stop him."

"No!" Ariel exclaims. "Then everyone will know we are clones. Our lives will be ruined."

"She's right," I say to Emma.

"My father always says you have to do the right thing for the right reason — never mind the consequences. And we don't know what the consequences will be."

"We do," I say. "CNN and the tabloids will take over our lives. We'll never have another normal day."

"And what about Eve?" Ariel interjects. "He could hurt her if he thinks it's all about to come out. She'd be a hindrance to him and he'd leave her to die."

"That's true, too," I agree.

"If Dr. Mullen is charged, couldn't our parents be charged also?" Ariel asks, bringing up a subject I prefer not to think about. "I mean, they paid for his work and they were going to have me used for spare parts for Miranda. Couldn't that get them in trouble with the police?"

I sit and think. I know that what Emma says is true. But how can I doom Ariel to a life as a lab rat? Because that's what she'll become. If I'm honest, I don't want that for myself either. Is that so wrong? And Ariel has a point about Eve. She may be an innocent dupe in all this. Or she may not be involved at all — left to die by Dr. Mullen. And then there's the question of my parents. I'm mad at them, but mad enough to send them to jail?

Just then my phone rings.

"Hello?" I say after grabbing it out of the knapsack.

"Miranda?"

"Eve?"

"I've escaped! I'm, I'm at a drugstore . . . "

"Where?"

"Hang on," and there is a pause. "At the mall at 111 and Washington," she says.

"Stay there," I say. "Don't move." I hang up. "Emma, can you call your brother? Think he'd come get us in the van? Eve's escaped, and she's in La Quinta. And I don't think I have the strength to ride her double all the way back to the ranch after that little gas episode."

Emma reaches for the phone. And I wonder if we are picking up a friend or an enemy.

Chapter 6

While we wait for Ben, we discuss how to explain Eve to him. Soon he drives up and helps us stow our bikes in the back of the van.

Emma tells him the story we've come up with. "Look, Ben," she says, "this is a secret. Not from Mom and Dad. As soon as they get home we'll tell them — just from your friends."

"Why?" he asks. Ben is sixteen, so Emma and I know lots of his friends from school. Some of them are even hot.

"Well it's all about this custody battle. See, Ariel has a twin. And when she came here . . ."

"I thought she was an orphan — your cousin," he says to me.

"She *is* my cousin," I answer. "But her father isn't dead. He took the other twin. And he raised her."

"Weird."

"Yeah," I continue, "and here's the thing. Apparently my mom hated her dad and they haven't ever spoken. So Eve, that's the twin, found out about Ariel a month ago, and she's run away and come here. But it has to be secret!"

"I don't like this," Ben says. "Her dad will be worried sick. The police will be involved."

"No. Because she told him she's going to stay with a friend here, and she's calling him every day. He thinks it's some kind of school exchange thing."

Ben tilts his head and looks at us all.

"Okay. That's the stupidest thing I've ever heard. What's the real story?"

"She's a clone," Emma sighs.

"Emma!" I exclaim.

But Ben laughs.

"Fine, don't tell me. I just hope you guys know what you're doing. Guess it can't be that bad if you're going to tell Mom and Dad. Let's go get this weirdo freak twin clone."

I smile weakly. We head down 111 and after a few minutes, sure enough, there is Eve, standing alone, peering around furtively. She looks just like Ariel — and she should, being the same age and an exact clone. She doesn't look sick either, which is a relief. She's dressed in a sleeveless white shift, no doubt something the nurses put her in.

She practically leaps into the van as we pull up. I'm at one window, Ariel slides over to the middle, and Eve buckles up beside Ariel. Emma twists around from the front seat. "Are you all right?"

Eve impulsively throws her arms around Ariel. "I am now," she says. "Let's get out of here." I reach over and squeeze her hand, so relieved to simply see her alive!

We drive away, none of us able to say much because of Ben. He's blaring his music anyway, so we all just settle in and rest as he drives us back to my house.

"I'll come get you at dinnertime," he says to Emma. "Mom and Dad will be back — we're ordering in."

"Thanks Ben," Emma says. "You can be a fairly decent brother when you try."

He grins. "See you."

As we get into the house, Emma says to me, "I wonder if he likes you."

"*Me?*"

"Yes, you. Ben never does me favours. Why would he start now?"

Ben is very cute. Curly black hair, tall, a bit gangly and a few too many zits, but all in all not unacceptable. And more importantly, he's a nice guy. Funny. Smart. A little naive. He'd never go out with me if he found out what I was. I grimace. "I don't think you'd want your brother hooked up with a freak."

"You aren't," she objects, giving me a gentle slap on the arm.

Meanwhile, Eve and Ariel haven't stopped talking. Emma and I follow them into the kitchen. Everyone grabs lemonade, and we raid the fridge — cold chicken and pasta salad and muffins. I'm not sure where Lorna is. As I watch Eve and see how happy she is to be with us, I push away the thought that she might have been in on setting us up. I observe her without her noticing, and there is nothing guilty or furtive about her behaviour.

We sit and gobble down our food. Finally, now sure I won't faint from hunger, I say to

Eve gently, "How are you feeling?"

She shakes her head. "Sometimes I feel fine. Sometimes I don't."

"And you don't know how sick you are?" Emma asks.

"No," she answers.

"How did you get away?" I ask.

"It wasn't hard," she answers, "once I put my mind to it. I crawled out the window. It was easy to break the lock."

"Why would Dr. Mullen bring you back here?" I ask.

"It seems you escaped pretty easily," Emma adds. "What happened to your nurses?"

"They were both in the kitchen or living room when I got out, I think," she says. "Why?"

"Because we were just at that house looking for you. It was empty. No nurses. And we nearly got killed, or at the very least knocked out, by some very nasty gas."

Eve stares at us. "But that's horrible. Why would they do that? It must have been some sort of accident."

"Have you seen the news?" I say.

"No."

I store that at the back of my mind, remembering the TV still on in the living room. But if her story is true and she's been confined to her room, then she wouldn't have seen it.

"Dr. Mullen's made a new clone. A boy," I explain. "And he's announced it to the world. I think he wants to get rid of the rest of us."

For a moment Eve doesn't speak. "It's possible," she says, reluctantly. "When he found out he had me and not his perfect Ariel, he was very angry."

We all sit for a moment in silence.

"I still think you need to come forward and tell people," Emma says to me.

"No!" Eve exclaims.

I stare at her in surprise. That's the most emotion she's shown since we found her.

"Why not?"

She seems to try to force herself to calm down. "Think what would happen to you and Ariel," she says.

"I know, I am thinking about it," I say.

"At least you won't be dead," Emma says, her voice low and intense.

"Maybe we'll wish we were," I retort. "And who knows, all the publicity might ruin our lives and still not protect us."

"But maybe it's not even about that," Emma says. "Maybe it's just about exposing him. He's dangerous. The world should know."

"Before we decide about that," I say, "we'd better decide what to do about Eve."

"In what way?" Eve asks.

"Do we let Mother and Father know you are here?"

"I don't think they liked me very much," Eve says.

"I think they may still be in touch with Dr. Mullen," I add. "I don't trust them. I think we should keep you a secret from them."

"She could come and live with us," Emma suggests. "It would be good because my dad could take care of her if she's sick and we could tell people who ask that she's Ariel. And Mom and Dad already know all about her . . . "

"That's a great solution," I say to Emma. "Eve, is that okay with you?"

Before she can answer, the phone rings. I answer. It's Mother.

"We're in New York," she says. "We'll be back late tonight. How are you, dear?"

"I'm fine," I say.

"Miranda, you *couldn't* be fine."

"See you later," I say.

"See you later," she echoes.

"My parents will be home later tonight," I report. "No doubt they'll find a way to make everything worse."

"They always do what they think is best for you," Ariel says in their defence.

"Or what's best for them," I say. "Think about it. Without their money and support Dr. Mullen would never have been able to create any of us. And perhaps be ready to kill us now. And why did they do it? They were selfish. They couldn't deal with Jessica's death. It wasn't about her and her life. It was about *them*. I hate them!" I exclaim suddenly.

The others stare at me. Emma pats my hand. "You couldn't hate them if part of you didn't love them, too," she says softly.

"That's what you think," I say, not wanting to admit that she might be right. "Listen, I'm hot — anyone want to go for a swim?"

"Me!" Ariel exclaims.

"Sure," Emma grins.

"Eve?"

"I'll dangle my feet," she says. "My head's hurting a bit."

Emma leaves a suit here for just such occasions. And soon we're splashing around trying to forget all we have to deal with, and the fact that someone may be trying to get rid of us!

* * *

Mother and Father arrive home around eleven that night. Eve is safely over at Emma's.

After all the hellos, Father excuses himself and goes into his den. Mother goes to shower. I listen at the door of the den. I *have* to! They still can't be trusted.

"I demand you meet with us to discuss this," I hear Father saying. "Don't think I can't still hurt you. You'd better find a time and a place to meet. Just remember who bankrolled all of this for you. And now Adam's family will be making millions: book deals, movie deals, sales to newspapers! And us? We funded your entire research, for heaven's sake, and we're practically broke!"

Dr. Mullen must answer back, and then Father says, "I know we didn't want it to come out. For one thing, there would be a lot of awkward questions about the other clones, wouldn't there." He listens. "That's true, we didn't want to move. But you owe us."

Another silence. "You can't tell me they aren't sharing some of that book and movie deal with you." He pauses again. "Then don't take it out of their cut, take it out of yours." And another pause. "Because you don't want all your secrets out, do you?" Pause. "No, we don't either. Fine. Tomorrow. Three o'clock."

I walk into the room. Father looks at me. "How much did you hear?"

"All of it. Why are you even negotiating with him? He'll stop at nothing — even murder. You can't trust him!" I plunk myself down in one of the thick leather chairs. "I think Dr. Mullen is behind the things that have been happening to me," I state. "He's trying to discredit me and our whole family."

"I don't suppose there's a better explanation," Father says. "I know you could never do those things, Miranda. Unless Ariel did them. Or a fourth clone. Or even Eve," he adds.

"No, Eve is sick, remember?" I say. "And Ariel didn't do it!" I'm almost completely positive. Of course she wasn't affected by the gas and we were . . . but no, she's the one who saved us! Oh, this is driving me mad! Now I'm even suspecting Ariel!

Father comes over to me and pats me on the shoulder. "Don't worry, Miranda, we'll take care of this," he says. "And no matter what, we've signed the deal on this new venture, so we should be able to get by."

Mother comes into the room. "And believe me, Miranda, no one is going to hurt you," she says, her voice grim, pulling her robe tight. "You can be sure of that."

I wish I could believe them.

I hurry off to my room to call Emma.

"So?" I ask.

"Well, they were a little surprised to see Eve, to say the least."

"Are they okay with it?"

"They are not too happy about Mullen resurfacing. I didn't tell them about the whole gas thing. You know them. I'd never be let out again on my own."

"Right," I say. "I get it. Won't mention it around them."

"Uh, listen, Miranda."

"What?"

"My dad really thinks you need to go public with this. Even without knowing what Mullen tried to do to us, he thinks the guy is dangerous." She pauses. I know something is up.

"Spill."

"He says if you won't tell, he might have to."

I feel the heat rising in my cheeks. "He'd do that? I thought I could trust him! He's the only one I *can* trust! Why would he do that against my wishes?"

"Because he's the adult. And he says sometimes the adult has to make the tough decision, if he knows it's the right one."

I try to think. "Okay, I get that. Ask him to give me just a few more days, all right? I need to think it all through."

"That should be good enough for him for now," she replies. "I'm sorry, Miranda, I know you don't need more on your plate."

"Hey, this is all part of it, isn't it? Meantime my dad is busy negotiating with Mullen."

"No!"

"Oh, yes."

"How can he still trust him?"

"My parents refuse to see reality as it is.

They have their own version. They make their own reality," I sigh. "And aren't I living proof of that?"

"Too true. So I better go make sure Eve is settled. Try to get some sleep."

"You, too. See you in the morning."

I hang up the phone and then sit where I am on my bed for the longest time, staring into space. What else might Dr. Mullen have planned?

Chapter 7

Monday morning and we're back at school. I'm nervous. I'm not sure what's going to happen next. Someone is going to try to frame me? Kill me?

Emma and I sit in English class but I can't concentrate. I keep replaying the conversation yesterday between Father and Dr. Mullen. Even though Father's deal went through, he still wants part of Mullen's money. Is it just greed, or is he that worried about my future health? Father certainly isn't interested in stopping or exposing Dr. Mullen. But why should he be? He was Mullen's first supporter. He made all this possible. On the other hand, Emma's dad thinks we need to tell the world because it's the only way to stop Mullen. But he does admit that since the world now knows about Mullen, maybe Ariel and Eve and I, and our well-being, are more important. He certainly doesn't want to ruin our lives.

Great! Now it's all clear as a desert sandstorm. If I tell, my parents could go to jail. I mean, can I live with that? And Ariel and me, well, our lives as we know them are done. So maybe it's best just to let Father get as much money out of Dr. Mullen as he can, start over, and pretend everything is normal. Something inside me says that all sounds very logical — but then no one will ever find out what an evil man Dr. Mullen is and how close Ariel came to being killed, like she wasn't human at all. No one will ever know the problems Eve and I have had, physically for sure — rare genetic diseases and all — but also mentally. I mean, growing up a freak isn't the funnest thing in the entire world. And worrying all the time: every time you get a headache — is it a brain tumour? First grey hair — premature aging? First depression about something — have you gone nuts? Dr. Mullen makes it all look so, so, *perfect*. But Eve isn't perfect. And I've already almost died once. And . . .

The fire alarm interrupts my thoughts. Everyone in the class groans. Grumbling is heard everywhere as we all file out, figuring it's some kind of drill and we'll have to stand outside under the hot sun. Until we smell the smoke, that is. Then we hurry.

Once outside, the grapevine works fast. Sue comes over to me and Emma. "Someone exploded something in chem lab." I roll my eyes. Honestly, at least once a year someone manages to do that.

"On purpose!" she adds.

"What do you mean?" I ask.

"The lab was empty. Someone went in and did something."

"Let's find Ariel," I say to Emma. The fire trucks have just pulled up and the firefighters are rushing into the school.

We find Ariel hanging out with her friends, chatting, enjoying the break.

"What's up?" she asks.

I have to smile. Only a short time ago she would have said: What is the problem? Or, Why have you searched me out?

"Nothing," I say. "Just wanted to say hello."

She gave me that little sister look, like, Okay, you've said hello, now stop embarrassing me. Emma and I take the hint and leave. At least I know she's fine. They can't leave us out baking in the sun for too long — it's 120 degrees today — so as soon as the firefighters have everything under control the bell rings and we're let back in.

I'm not at my desk more than five minutes when: *"Will Miranda Martin please come to the office?"*

I groan. "I didn't do it!" I exclaim to the class. Everyone laughs. They were all with me the whole time, so that's a pretty safe bet. And funnily enough no one really believes I wrote the graffiti. Well, a few kids always like to think the worst so I did get *some* grief. But mostly everyone thinks I'm too much of a goody-goody. It almost upsets me to think that they couldn't even *imagine* me doing something bad. Who wants to be that predictable?

Still, when I get to the office Mrs. MacKay motions me to go straight in to Mrs. Dean. I get into her office and she shuts the door.

"The cameras show you coming out of the lab just before the explosion."

"Mr. Gorden will tell you differently," I say, heart sinking. There *must* be a fourth clone!

"I was in class the entire time."

"He'll confirm that? No bathroom breaks? Nothing?"

"Nothing."

"Can you explain how you can be in two places at once?"

"No." Well, I could, of course, but I won't.

"Miranda, you must have figured out a way to slip out of Mr. Gorden's class without him noticing. The camera doesn't lie."

"What was I wearing?"

She looks at my clothes.

"Not that."

"I rest my case. Can I see the tape?"

She puts it in and I look. Bulky top, overalls — as if I'd ever wear overalls — baseball cap. Very similar to me, but not me.

"Maybe someone has it in for me," I suggest. "Dress like me, you know, set me up."

"Why?" she asks.

I shrug.

Mrs. Dean looks unconvinced. She must think I slipped out of class, changed clothes . . .

"Why would I want to do it?" I say.

"You tell me," she answers.

"I wouldn't. And I didn't do the graffiti

either. Or the shoplifting."

"Well, this is all very odd, Miranda."

"I know, Mrs. Dean," I say.

"You can go."

At lunch Emma and I try to work out what is going on. But we're interrupted by Ben.

"Hey," he says, "can I join?"

"Sure," I say.

Emma looks surprised. "You are gracing us with your presence? To what do we owe this honour?"

"Actually, I thought I should tell you I saw Eve at school today. She was supposed to stay home, wasn't she?"

"Are you sure it was Eve, not Ariel?" Emma asks.

"Pretty sure. She was wearing those over-alls of yours I think are so stupid, that's why I noticed."

I gasp. Eve? I'd forgotten Emma had those overalls.

"What would she be doing here?" Ben asks.

"Blowing up the chem lab?" I suggest. Ben smiles. He thinks I'm joking.

"When did you see her?" I ask.

"I was on an errand for Ms Jiminez during second period, and there she was. She disappeared around the corner before I could call her. I only saw her for a second, but like I said, I couldn't miss the stupid overalls."

Emma and I look at each other. We don't say anything while he's there. As soon as he leaves, which he kind of seems reluctant to do, hanging around talking and stuff, Emma grabs my wrist.

"Maybe there's not a fourth clone," she says quietly. "It makes sense. She's grown as tall as you, just like Ariel."

"Maybe," I agree. "But it *doesn't* make sense. Why would she do any of this?"

"We'd better find out, don't you think?"

"Yes, I do," I say. "Let's go now."

"No," Emma says. "You're in enough trouble. Call your mom and ask her if you can come over after school. We'll confront Eve then."

"Maybe we shouldn't confront her," I say. "Maybe she won't admit anything. Maybe we need to spy on her. Catch her in the act."

"You might be right," Emma agrees. "Otherwise she can just deny it all."

I shake my head. "I just don't understand," I say. "*Why* would she do it?"

"Could she regret her decision to take Ariel's place and go back to Dr. Mullen?"

"Why would she?" I ask. "He was her only hope, everyone else said she was incurable. And he might have succeeded."

"Or not," Emma says grimly. "Her headaches are back. What if she is sick? Really sick. And it's affecting her behaviour. Remember when she was first diagnosed with the brain tumour — the doctor said it could cause a change in personality."

"We don't know Eve very well," I say. "We don't really know what her personality is."

"She *is* a clone of you," Emma comments.

"So, does that mean her personality will be the same?" I challenge Emma. "Does that mean I'm the same as Jessica? Is Ariel the same as me?"

"We've gone over this before," Emma says. "I don't think so."

"And yet you don't think she could be bad because I'm good."

Emma grimaces. "Oh, I don't know what to think."

"No use speculating," I answer. "We'll have to watch her to find out."

"We may need to clue Ben in," Emma says. "I mean, how do we follow her if he won't drive us around?"

"I don't want Ben to know!" I object.

Her eyebrows rise. "You like him."

"I don't!"

"Otherwise you wouldn't care."

I change the subject. "How did Eve get here all the way from your house?"

"No clue," Emma answers. "Another reason to follow her."

"We'll just tell Ben we suspect her — we don't need to tell him the whole clone story."

"Okay," Emma agrees. "Call your mom and tell her you're coming over. We'll take it from there. What the heck is she playing at?" she adds.

"Let's just hope we can find out," I answer.

Chapter 8

We arrive at Emma's to find Eve all sweetness and light. She's wearing shorts, though, not overalls. Why would she try to blow up the lab? Was she trying to get me in trouble? Or was she trying to blow up the school and kill us all? Maybe this had nothing to do with getting me in trouble at all.

Ariel has gone home with Mother. It would look suspicious if Emma and I let her hang out with us. We don't want to raise any flags with Mother or Father.

I'm getting a little worried about just following Eve. What if she does something really dangerous and we can't stop her? On the other hand, I guess there still *could* be a fourth clone and Eve *might* be completely innocent. Emma and I have devised a plan to see if she'll give herself away.

"Emma and I need to study for a really important exam," I say to Eve. "Do you mind if we close the door and work right through till dinner?"

"No," she answers readily. "You go ahead. By the way, how was your day?"

"Oh, fine," I reply.

"Good," she says.

We've decided not to even mention the fire. Let her stew, if it's her.

"How was yours?" I ask.

"Boring. Just sat inside and watched TV and read."

Emma and I go into Emma's room and close the door. It's not more than five minutes later that Ben comes in. "She's snuck out of the house," he says.

He's agreed to spy on her for us — although he's getting more and more suspicious about who she is and what's going on.

"Will you take us to follow her?" I ask.

"Sure, come on," he says. "Mom, I'm just driving the girls to the mall," he calls to his mother.

"Be home by six for dinner," she calls back.

We head out in the van. Within a minute

we spot Eve. She's on Emma's bike and has gone about three blocks.

"Well, at least we know how she got to school, if it was her," I say.

She turns into one of the many mini malls. We follow at a discreet distance. She parks her bike in front of a big record store, locks it up, goes in. We hurry out of the van and follow her in. Each of us takes a different direction to track her down. I see her first.

She's looking up at the security camera. Then she takes a couple of CDs and drops them in her knapsack! She's obviously going to make a run for it and have the camera show it was me! I stalk over to her, grab the bag and empty it on the floor. About a dozen CDs fall out. I pick them up and put them back on the shelf. Then I take her wrist and drag her over to the front desk.

"Can I speak to the manager?"

Soon an older man shows up. So do Ben and Emma. Eve stands quietly, not looking surprised to see me or upset that I've got a grip of steel on her wrist.

"May I speak to you privately?" I ask the manager.

"Yes."

I loosen my grip on Eve. "Don't move," I order her.

The manager and I walk a little away from the others. I call on all my acting skills.

"Your security camera is going to show my cousin there," I point to Eve, "putting CDs in her knapsack. Please could you ignore it this once? She's here from out of town and trying to make friends. She got in with the wrong crowd and they dared her. I promise it won't happen again."

He stares at me for a moment, thinking. "She has to be banned from the store," he says, finally.

"Of course."

"All right."

"Thank you!"

I turn away from him and motion the others that it's time to go. Ben has a firm grip on Eve's arm. We collect her bike, throw it in the back of the van and get in. Ben drives us home.

None of us says a word. He parks in the driveway and Emma and I drag Eve into Emma's room. Ben tries to join us, saying, "Hey, I should get to hear what's going on!"

"We need to talk to her alone. Trust me on

this," Emma says, blocking Ben at the door.

Ben looks doubtful, but can tell by the tone of Emma's voice that she means it. He shrugs assent.

"Thanks," she says. "I promise I'll explain later."

"I'll hold you to that," he replies.

I shut the door and turn to Eve.

"Why?" I ask.

She flips her hair back and stares at me defiantly. "Why not?"

"Sit down," I order her.

"I prefer to stand."

Emma and I are standing too. I have my hands on my hips. I'm tempted to thump her.

"Did you have anything to do with the gas in the house?"

"How could I?"

"I don't know how. I'm asking you."

"Don't you think you found that house very easily?" She asks.

"Dr. Mullen wanted us to find it," I state.

"Maybe."

"You didn't warn us? You would have let us die?" I exclaim. "I can't believe it. You would-n't!"

"Oh, grow up," Eve snarls. "I had a choice

to make — me or you. And I chose me."

"But," Emma interrupts, "I don't understand. You've changed so much. You can't be
the same Eve that gave herself up for Ariel."
Emma turns to me. "She's probably not Eve
at all! She's the fourth clone and Eve is being
kept somewhere by Dr. Mullen."

"You go ahead and think that, if it makes
you feel better," Eve says.

"Is it true?" I ask. "Are you a fourth clone?"

"I doubt you'll believe me one way or the
other," she answers. "But I *am* Eve. And Dr.
Mullen gave me a choice: help him get you in
serious trouble, even get rid of you, and he'll
put all he's got into curing me. At first I
refused. Then I got sick. And sicker. And so I
agreed. He got me on this new experimental
drug. And he's going to make sure I'm okay."

"Eve," I say, "he might do the best he can —
if you can even trust him to do that. But it
doesn't mean he can cure you."

"I know," she says. "But it's my only chance.
And he doesn't want you and Ariel around to
mess up his business. You . . . were a mistake
he wants to forget."

"You mean Miranda and Ariel are proof of
his illegal activities. And what about you?"

Emma asks. "You're his worst failure. At least Ariel is as perfect as Adam. Don't you think he'll want to get rid of you first?"

"No!"

"Why not?"

For a moment she can't think of an answer. "Because he said," she finally answers lamely.

"And you grabbed at anything," I mutter, "because you were desperate."

"He was fascinated that I agreed," she says. "He said he didn't think my genetic programming would allow me to hurt you."

"He said that?" I say.

"Yes."

"Don't you get it?" I exclaim. "You're just another of his experiments. He wanted to see how far you'd go, to see if you could be a bad girl, his dark clone."

"That's not it!" she insists. "He's going to help me. And I can do it because I'm not programmed like you are to be the perfect good girl. Who wants to live like that?"

"But you are my clone!" I insist. "You are the same as me."

"Well then I've broken free! I'm an individual and you're trapped. You're stupid. You are a sitting duck for him right now."

"So are you!" I say.

"No, because I don't care if I have to live in a lab somewhere and have a secret life. I don't care as long as I can live. Who knows what the future will bring?"

Emma goes to the door. "We need to talk," she says to me. She turns to Eve. "You — you stay here. We can catch up to you in the van, so don't try to take off."

Emma grabs the phone and takes it with her.

She leads me out of her room and into the backyard, empty of brothers now because of the heat. "What on earth are we going to do?" she says.

"I don't know! I think we need to tell your dad."

"I'm not so sure," Emma says. "He'll freak. He'll expose Dr. Mullen and your parents before he lets anything happen to me or you or Ariel. And then you won't be able to decide anything."

"I don't think they've left me any choice," I say. "I've been trying to protect Ariel, and my parents and me, of course. But maybe by saying nothing I've put us in more danger. I've let Dr. Mullen get in a position now where even if I say anything they'll just say oh, she's just a troubled kid. Blowing up labs, shoplifting, vandalism — you know."

"Eve doesn't care if she hurts us, as long as she isn't hurt. She doesn't care at all how we feel," Emma says. "So she's very dangerous."

"But we can't let her hurt us," I say.

"How do we stop her? We can't lock her up," Emma points out.

"Maybe it's time to tell my father and mother. They've never cared about her. They'll have no compunction about making sure she can't hurt me or you or Ariel."

"I don't like it. They would hand her right back over to Dr. Mullen. And even though she trusts him . . ."

I add to her thought, "He's capable of anything. What if she *is* some kind of test for him and now that he has his data he'll just let her die. Or kill her."

The stars are coming out overhead, twinkling in the blue-black sky. I am truly at a loss. I don't know what to do. I feel paralyzed. Eve is not on my side, but I still care about what happens to her. How can I let her die?

"You know what my dad always says,"

Emma suggests. "Do what you believe is right. Sometimes it works out, sometimes it doesn't. You can't control that."

"But I know that if I come forward and let the world know about Dr. Mullen, our lives as we know them are over. So I know it won't work out."

"But you also know that not saying anything isn't working out either, is it?"

"No," I agree, "it certainly isn't."

A scream from inside the house stops all conversation. It's Eve.

Chapter 9

Emma's dad reaches Eve before we do. He's just back from work. Eve is holding her head, screaming in pain. Dr. Green talks to her in a soothing voice. He looks in her eyes. Then he says, "She needs to get to the hospital. Come on. I'll drive."

It's only five minutes away to the Desert Oasis where he has privileges. We all pile into Dr. Green's car, Eve in back with me, Emma in front with her dad. Eve is whimpering from pain. I hold her hand. She squeezes mine so hard it hurts. When we get to the hospital she is whisked away and Emma and I are left to wait. I'm feeling so numb and confused I don't know what to think. Finally Dr. Green comes and finds us.

He makes us sit, and he perches on a small

table across from us. He clears his throat. "I'm sorry to have to tell you this, but Eve is a very sick girl. Her cancer has returned. We can't operate because of where it's situated. Has she been behaving normally?"

Emma looks at me. I nod.

"No," Emma sighs. "Not at all. She's been purposely trying to get Miranda in trouble."

"Well, tumours in the area where hers is located can be associated with behavioural changes."

"Is there any hope for her?" I ask.

He shakes his head.

"How long?" Emma asks.

"We can never say," he replies. "But we're talking days or weeks, not months or years."

"Can she come home with us?" Emma asks.

"For a while," he answers. "But soon she'll need more care than we can give her." He puts his hands over ours. "I'm sorry, girls. I know how hard this is."

"Dr. Green," I ask, "is this something that could happen to me, or Ariel?"

"I can't tell you that," he replies. "It may have to do with the cloning, it may not. I'm sure of one thing — you need to be monitored more closely than a," he pauses, "well, than most teenagers."

He was going to say normal, I know he was.

"We're stabilizing Eve with some strong drugs. She'll stay overnight."

"Can we see her?" I ask.

"Not now," he says. "You'll see her tomorrow after school. She'll be released then. Come on, let's get home and get some food in you two."

Jewish mothers have nothing on Jewish fathers. Emma and I both exchange a small smile despite ourselves. Food cures everything.

We do feel a bit better after we've eaten. My mother is due to pick me up at nine so Emma and I don't have a lot of time to talk. We go back outside, the stars blanketing the sky now, the moon a beautiful crescent.

I sit on a rocker and she lies down in a hammock.

"And she thought she was free!" I say. "Instead her tumour was making her do bad things."

"You're too nice," Emma says.

"What do you mean?"

"Just what I said. Say her tumour does change her. She can still choose! She didn't have to try to destroy you. Come on. We all have free choice."

I stop to think about that. "I'm not so sure. I'm engineered to be smart and strong and according to Dr. Mullen, good. And hey, guess what? I'm all of those things."

"Yeah," Emma says, "and you could be the biggest snob in the entire world, but you aren't. You could be at the top of the school with your looks and smarts. But instead you hang out with normal types like me and Sue. And it's not like your parents exactly set the best example — they've always given you everything you ever asked for."

"They loved me," I say softly.

"They still do. Maybe that makes up for everything. No one has ever loved Eve, have they? I mean, you love Ariel and she knows it and look at what a great kid she's turning into. So Eve doesn't have love, she goes for . . . I don't know, survival?"

"But when she sacrificed herself for Ariel, tricking Mullen into taking her instead . . . "

"Yeah," Emma says, "she probably thought we'd love her for that. But then she ends up with Mullen and he only cares about her for what she can deliver. For whatever use she can be to him. And if that's all she can get — well, that'll be what she goes for."

"I hate to say it," I admit, "but I think you're right. We may have limits, but within those we can choose. And now I have the biggest choice of my life, and Ariel's, to make. I just wish there was a way we could expose Dr. Mullen without also exposing me and Ariel, and my parents."

"Maybe there is," Emma says.

"I don't think so."

"Come on. You're so smart. You must be able to think of something."

"There's nowhere we can hide, though, is there? I mean in the olden days people with secrets would go to Europe or London. But the press is even worse over there. The first clones — we'll be tracked every moment of our lives."

"But that'll calm down after a while, right?"

"Yes, but everyone'll know. All our friends. Any new friends I'll make. I'll be looked at like some sort of freak."

"I don't look at you that way."

"How many of you are out there?"

"You might be surprised."

Dr. Green comes outside and interrupts us. "Girls?"

"Yes?" Emma says.

"I have some disturbing news."

Emma sits up. "What?"

"Eve has disappeared. She's not in the hospital."

My heart sinks. Now what?

"Where could she have gone?" I ask. "I thought she was all drugged up."

"She was," Dr. Green says. "I'm worried about her. She's drugged, she's aggressive. She may not be safe to be around."

"Ariel," I say to myself. Without another word I get up and race to the phone. I dial home. Mother answers. "Is Ariel there?" I ask.

"No, she went out with a friend," Mother answers.

"Who?"

"I'm not sure."

"What do you mean?" I yell. "How could you not know?"

"She said one of her friends from school was picking her up and that she'd be back soon."

"You'd never let me do that," I accuse. "You still don't care about Ariel, do you, even after all this time!"

"I'm trying, Miranda," Mother says, her voice trembling with anger. "I didn't ask to have Ariel here."

No, I wanted to say, you were just keeping her for parts. But what was the point? I'd said that many times, and it didn't change anything. I hang up and try Ariel on her cell.

To my relief she answers right away.

"Ariel!"

"Hi, Miranda!"

"Where are you?"

"I'm with Eve."

My heart is in my throat. In fact my throat goes so dry I can hardly get out the next sentence.

"Where are you?"

"Oh, I'm not sure. She came and got me in a cab, said you needed us both. We're — where are we anyway?"

Suddenly the line goes dead.

"Ariel? Ariel?"

I turn to Emma and Dr. Green. "Eve has Ariel. She's taking her somewhere."

"Why?" Dr. Green asks.

"Yes, why?" Emma echoes.

"She saved Ariel only a few months ago," I say. "She knows that Ariel will trust her absolutely. I don't know why she's gone after her, but somehow as soon as I heard Eve was gone I knew she would. Oh, why didn't I think to warn Ariel?"

"None of us thought Eve would be going anywhere," Dr. Green reminded me.

"We all forget how strong Ariel and Eve and I are. Drugs that would knock out a normal kid probably just took away her headache and made her feel well enough to get busy," I say.

"But get busy with what?" Emma says.

"I wish I knew," I say. "We'd better find out soon. If she hurts Ariel, I'll, I'll . . . "

"What?" says Emma. "Kill her? Seems to me she doesn't have much to lose." Emma turns to her dad. "Did you tell her about the cancer?"

"I did. She said not to worry. Dr. Mullen would fix it. She was delirious, of course."

"Fix it. Dr. Mullen *would* fix it or *did* fix it?"

"Would," Dr. Green says.

"She knows about the new tumour," I say.

"And Dr. Mullen has promised to cure her again. As long as she does as he asks. And at the same time he can watch her and see what she's willing to do, to avoid dying."

"That's what I'm worried about," Emma says. "Just how bad is she willing to be?"

Chapter 10

"Why would she take Ariel?" I say, almost to myself.

"Why did Dr. Mullen want Ariel last time?" Dr. Green offers. "Her genetic code."

"Plus," I add, another thought occurring to me, "without Ariel I can't tell the world about me being a clone. She and Eve are the only proof I have."

"That's it!" Emma exclaims. "Without Ariel you are just a nut who shoplifts and writes graffiti on walls."

"So he very well might kill her," I say grimly.

"I think we can't rule it out. We'll have to call the police and put out an Amber alert," says Dr. Green.

The phone rings and makes us jump a

mile. Dr. Green answers. He listens. "Yes Eve, I understand." Pause. "Eve, you are very sick. I really think . . . " He stares at the phone.

"She hung up."

"What did she say?" Emma asks anxiously.

"She said that Ariel won't be hurt — but if we call the police, she'll be killed. And we'll never find the body."

"This might call for my parents to get involved." I say, knowing now that I waited too long to make my decision. Too long. "They are the ones in touch with Dr. Mullen. They're the only ones who might be able to negotiate with him."

In fact my mother is due to get me any moment, so I grab my stuff, say a quick good-bye, and promise to keep Emma and her dad up to date.

When Mother gets me she starts to quiz me as soon as I get into the car. "Why all the worry about Ariel?" she asks.

"Let's wait till we get home," I say. "Dad will need to be involved."

"Dad?" she says. "I haven't heard you call him that in months."

She's right. Maybe that talk with Emma softened me a bit. But just a bit. I still think.

that they were selfish, creating me so they wouldn't have to deal with their grief. But it's also true what I said — they *have* loved me.

When we're home, we sit down in the kitchen. Mother puts on the kettle for tea. I grab a lemonade. And suddenly I start to cry. Ariel loves lemonade. And I might never see her again. Father tentatively puts an arm around my shoulder — I've been so angry at him I haven't so much as let him kiss my cheek. But now I find myself sobbing into his embrace.

"Miranda," he says, his voice soothing, "what it is it? It can't be that bad."

"It is," I say, hiccuping. "It is. Dr. Mullen has Ariel. We're never going to see her again." And then I tell them about Eve and about everything that's happened up till now.

"You were right to tell us," Father says.

"You should have told us about Eve right away," Mother exclaims. "Why, you could be dead right now! Oh, I'd like to get my hands on Mullen."

"He'll be here in an hour," Father says.

"What?" I exclaim.

"You're joking," Mother says.

"No. It's what I arranged yesterday. He's

agreed to split some of his profits with us in exchange for our silence. We're meeting to iron out the deal."

"You can't trust him," I say. "With all of us out of the way, he'd be free and clear."

"Yes," Father says, "I can see that. And with Ariel gone, there's no proof that you are a clone, and so he doesn't need to pay us anything."

"He won't come," I predict. "He doesn't have to now."

We sit and wait. But by eleven it's clear that he won't be coming. No call, no show. I wash up and get into bed. The whole house feels empty. I lie awake and another horrible thought occurs to me. I'm home free. Dr. Mullen will never admit I'm a clone. Ariel is gone. If I agree to keep quiet, and can convince Dr. Mullen I'm no threat, I could probably have a totally normal life with no one suspecting anything. Even Ben . . .

I call Emma. "Emma do you realize that if I do nothing now, I could be safe forever?"

"I've been sitting by the phone waiting for you to call!" she scolds me. "My dad is still talking about an Amber alert."

"I'm sorry. I'm not thinking straight. Dr.

Mullen was supposed to come here — he never showed. My parents can't help. If we're going to find Ariel, you and I will have to do it."

"Then we will," she answers.

"How? Where do we start?"

"Well, we could start at that house in La Quinta where Eve was living before."

"But why would she go back there?"

"Do you have any better ideas?"

"No. Will Ben take us?"

"I'll ask. Tomorrow after school?"

"Sure."

"Maybe you should think about it," Emma suggests. "You *are* free and clear now."

"I know," I say. "It crossed my mind, but I couldn't live with myself. If Ariel hadn't given me half her liver I'd be dead now. I can't just let Mullen take her. She's my sister now."

"Yeah. I know," Emma sighs. "My dad's calling the police first thing in the morning, so we'll want to act fast."

I lie in the dark after we hang up, unable to sleep. Why didn't I speak out when I could have? I told myself I was trying to protect Ariel but the truth is, I was scared. I was scared of the circus my life would become. I was scared of being labeled a freak. I was just plain scared. Of course the right thing was to stop Dr. Mullen. Stand up to him. Not so easy when you're scared though, is it? Guess that's how bullies and dictators get so powerful. No one wants to stand up to them. I see why now. The trouble is, what happens later is even scarier.

Tears trickle down my cheeks. Poor Ariel. She didn't deserve any of this. And neither did I. At this moment I wish I'd never been — well — created! But I have been, and now I have to deal. *I won't let you go without a fight,* I vow to Ariel before I fall into a troubled sleep.

I don't know what wakes me up, but I am suddenly wide awake. I look at the clock by my bed. It's one a.m.

Dr. Mullen was supposed to be here at eleven. He didn't show. But why make an appointment like that if you aren't going to be in town? Maybe he'd made the appointment with dad as an insurance policy. If he couldn't snatch Ariel, he'd make a deal with dad. If he could grab her, no deal needed!

I grab the phone. Emma answers, groggy.

"Emma, can you get Ben to drive us?"

"Yes, I said I would."

"No! Now!"

"Now?"

"Yes."

"Why?"

"Think about it. Dr. Mullen has Ariel. Alive. She and Eve are proof that I'm a clone. Eve's going to die soon anyway. I'm not perfect. Maybe he doesn't need Ariel alive. He kills her, uses her tissue to create more clones. He doesn't snatch me because I'm not perfect; I've almost died once already. I'm defective. And without her I can't tell on him. Which means he'll be extracting the DNA soon. Maybe even tonight. He'll need an operating room," I say, the words tumbling out. "And there was one all set up at the La Quinta house."

"Okay," Emma says. "I'll be there soon as I can." She pauses. "Should we call the police?"

"No way! If we're wrong, it's just one more thing that shows how crazy I am."

Emma hangs up. I throw on a pair of jeans and a sweatshirt and sneakers. I creep down the hallway, only to see my dad sitting in the kitchen drinking a scotch. He looks pretty worried. I wonder where Mother is.

"Miranda?"

Oh great! Right behind me!

I try to seem casual as I turn around.

"Yeah?"

"What are you doing?"

"Nothing, just getting some water."

She's in her nightgown and looks like she's about to go to bed. "In your jeans?"

"I couldn't sleep. Thought I'd sit outside for a bit."

She nods.

I go into the kitchen and take a glass and fill it with water from the fridge.

"Can't sleep either?" Father asks.

"No."

"Want some company?" The look of hope in his eyes is sad.

"No thanks, Dad," I answer. "I just need to sit for a while. I'll be on the porch."

He seems a little mollified — at least I called him Dad.

I take my glass and go out onto the patio off the kitchen. I sit on a chair where Dad can see me. I can also see the driveway from here.

Then he comes outside anyway!

"Miranda?" He sits down.

"Yeah?"

"None of this is your fault."

I don't want to fight with him. Or talk to him at all. He can't see Emma and Ben!

"I know."

"You do?"

"Yes." I don't, but I need to get rid of him. I didn't do the right thing when I could have. But neither did he. And I am his daughter — sort of.

"Look Dad, I'd just like to sit out here alone for awhile. Okay?"

"Sure," he says, uncertainly. "But don't beat yourself up."

The words just blurt out despite my resolve not to talk to him. "No, but I should learn to take responsibility when I'm wrong. Shouldn't I? Or is that something you'd rather not talk about?"

"It's something I'd like to talk about. But I don't admit I was wrong to make you — look at you. We love you so much. We could never agree with you that it was a mistake." He stares down into his glass and sounds like he's going to cry.

"Sure, Dad," I say, "I see that."

"You do?"

"Yes. I mean," and to my surprise I think I mean it, "I'm glad I'm alive. Even though a little while ago I felt the opposite. I guess I wouldn't have missed this for the world."

He smiles. "Thank you, Miranda. Thank you."

"Now can I just . . . "

"Oh. Right. Don't get cold."

It's about 80 degrees, so that's unlikely.

"I won't."

"And don't stay out too long. School tomorrow."

"Sure."

"You're free and clear now, you know," he says. "You can be a normal teenager. No one will ever have to know your secret."

"Yeah. I realized that a while ago."

"How does it make you feel?"

"I'd be so happy."

"You'd be . . . "

"If not for Ariel."

He knows this is where it gets dangerous. "I'll go in now."

And just in time — because I can see the van turning into the drive.

Chapter 11

I slip into the back of the van and close the door as quietly as I can. Ben pulls out onto the street and stops.

"That's it," he says. "I'm not going any farther until I know what's happening. I have the distinct feeling that Mom and Dad should know about this."

"If we tell you, we'd have to kill you." I try a lame joke.

He calls me on it. "Not even close to funny enough — come on now. I'm the big brother. I don't intend to get my little sister into trouble."

Emma twists in her seat to look at me. I shrug. She knows what that means. My heart races. How will he react?

"The thing is," Emma says, "we really

weren't joking before. Mom and Dad know about this. Miranda really is a clone. So is Ariel. So is Eve. Dr. Mullen is behind it all. And now he's kidnapped Ariel and we think she's in danger — like he might kill her."

"Emma!" Ben exclaims. "It's late. I've got an English test in the morning. This isn't funny."

"She's telling the truth," I say. "I didn't want you to know. I didn't want you to think of me as a freak."

Something in the tone of my voice must make him reconsider. "You're serious?"

"Deadly," I reply.

"But it's impossible."

"Well, you know it isn't. You've seen Dr. Mullen on TV with the new clone. I was his first."

That clinches it.

"Man oh man," he says. He pauses. "So shouldn't we be calling the police?"

"Yes," I agree. "We should call the police if we can find Ariel and Dr. Mullen and Eve. But a wild goose chase won't convince anyone. I've got my cell. The minute we find them we'll call the police. And the newspapers. I've got the number of the *Los*

Angeles Times with me. Hopefully, once the secret is out we'll be safe."

"You've decided?" Emma says.

"I should have done it days ago. Now it might be too late to save Ariel," I say, trying to fight back tears. I tap Ben on the shoulder. "Can we go?"

"Where to?" he asks.

We give him directions. As we drive through the night I'm reminded of the time last year, right around now, when I got sick. I was terrified, sure I was going to die. And now I'm terrified all over again. One way or another, everything is about to change.

The lights of the cars whiz past as they did a year ago. I put my window down and feel the air on my face, breathe in the fragrance of the night flowers and lemon trees. This won't be the last time I'm going to be afraid. But I make a vow to myself — that I won't live in fear. I'll try not to make my decisions based on fear. By doing that I've actually made my worst fear come true. Well, hopefully, not yet. Hopefully Ariel is still alive. And she's somewhere we can find her. I didn't do a very good job protecting her.

Ben speaks and startles me out of my reverie.

"I just want you to know something, Miranda," he says.

"Yes?"

"Well, like, that, you're still who you are. You're not a freak or anything. Not really. I mean so you were made differently. Don't get hung up on it." He almost sounds like he's trying to convince himself. "*Does* it make you different?" he continues.

"Who knows?" I say. "The animals they've cloned suffer from premature aging. I could get diseases that older people get, like osteoporosis, even cancer. I've already nearly died once."

"Yeah, well, it sucks, but kids get cancer all the time. I mean, you'll just have to deal as it comes, but we all do, right?"

"Right," I say. And now the tears do come. Why is he being so nice?

He can tell I'm upset so he turns on the CD and plays whatever's in there. His mom must have been in the van, because it's a Frank Sinatra disc. Kinda soothing, actually.

We have Ben park near the back of the golf course and start out on foot. The moon sheds a weak light on the course, enough at least for us to move slowly toward the streets, and once on the street I can easily remember the way. "What's the plan?" Ben asks, as we stop just by the house.

"We don't exactly have one," I whisper. "We're just going to try to see if they could be here."

"We need a plan," he insists. "I should go in, you two stay out here."

"No!" I exclaim. "No way. I can get away with being there — if I'm seen anyone could assume I'm Eve or Ariel — from a distance at least. I think I should go in alone. I'll set my cell to redial your number out here so I only have to push one button. If they're there, I'll dial. Then you call in the cavalry."

"It makes sense," Emma says. "One kid who looks like the others is a lot less of a chance. But how do we get you in?"

"And what if there are some tough guys in there and you never get a chance to call?" Ben asks.

"Well, obviously then you'll also know to get help."

"Fine. Two minutes," Ben says. "If you aren't out here in two, telling us that no one's there, then I'm calling the cops."

"Fair enough," I agree.

I walk up to the front door, expecting it to be locked. Then I figure I'll try all the windows. Then the back door. And if that fails — well, I'll just ring the doorbell and see if anyone answers. The place looks dark, but I know that could mean anything — they'd want it to look that way.

Heart pounding, I try the knob. Of course it's locked. I walk around until I get to the back of the house. I notice a sliding door — it must lead to the living room. I try it. No luck. I run back to the front.

"Ben," I say, "there's a sliding door. Can you help me open it?"

"I can," he says. "But it's probably rigged to an alarm."

"That's okay. So long as I get in — if everyone comes running at least we'll know something is up in there."

"Let's do it," Ben says.

The three of us hurry around to the back. Ben kicks the lock hard a few times until it snaps and we can push the door open. Sure enough an alarm goes off. I push some dark, heavy drapes back. Light floods the room and a nasty looking guy, big, dressed incongruously in a bright red Hawaiian shirt, slams out of one of the back rooms and marches into the living room.

"Get away," I hiss to Ben. "Hey," I call out, "someone was trying to get in here."

He stares at me. "I thought you were . . ." He looks over at the operating room.

"That guy just broke in here," I shout at the goon, "get after him or the whole plan is in danger!"

He hesitates for a moment, then takes off out the back door.

I hope Emma and Ben will be able to handle him. The alarm still ringing, I open the door to the small room.

"Get out of here!" about three people yell at once. "You're not sterile. Get out!"

Someone is on the table. They've already started cutting. There's a lot of blood. I race over to look at the face. Ariel! She's got a tube down her throat. I stare down at the incision.

Everyone is masked, but I'm pretty sure the short guy is Dr. Mullen.

"You have to stop!" I scream. "Stop!"

"It's too late for that," he says. "We're just

finishing. We only have her eyes left." It's him.

"What do you mean?"

"I mean kidneys, heart, lungs, liver. They're all on their way already. On a jet out of here. They're worth good money." My legs suddenly feel like jelly. I stagger.

"Get her out of here," Dr. Mullen orders.

Someone grabs my arm and pulls me out into the living room.

I shake them off and sink to the floor, gasping for breath. I feel sick. I put my head between my legs, try to stop shaking.

Tears are streaming down my face. Vaguely, through it all, I hear sirens blaring. And then I realize that Dr. Mullen will hear them. And he'll try to escape. *And that will not happen*. I look around. There's a large desk in a corner. With strength I didn't know I had, I push it in front of the door to his operating theatre. Then I place myself in front of it, ready to fight to keep them there if I need to.

Time seems to slow down. Someone is pushing against the door. Pushing harder. Harder. The desk is being pushed back. Pounding starts on the front door. I run over to it and scramble with the lock and fling open the door. It's the police!

"In there!" I shout, pointing. "Behind the desk!"

They push the desk away. The door flies open and Dr. Mullen, mask off, staggers out of the room, along with the others. I slip past them into the room and move over to Ariel's body. I stare down at her. They've dragged a sheet over her, but it's too horrible and I have to look away. When I do, I see a body on the other table. I walk over slowly, dreading what I'll see. Eve?

"Miranda?" A faint voice says.

"Eve?" I whisper.

"Ariel," she says. "That's Eve. You got here in time. Just like, just like, the cavalry."

I laugh and cry at the same time. She's hooked up to a drip in her arm.

"I was next. He was going to take some samples, and then, well, then I don't think he would have needed me anymore. Eve came to get me and she was laughing about how stupid you were. And then she brought me here. Where is she?"

"She's dead," I answer.

Ariel's eyes close.

"Someone help!" I yell.

A policeman hurries over. He talks into his shoulder piece.

"Is she going to be all right?" I ask him.

"EMS is on their way. We'll know soon."

I hold Ariel's hand.

Within a couple of minutes she's being checked by an EMS attendant, a young woman. "Looks like she's just sedated. It should wear off in a few hours."

From the next room I can hear Dr. Mullen protesting as the police take him away.

Is it over?

Or just beginning?

Chapter 12

Light bulbs flash. I'm almost blinded. Ariel is holding my hand so tightly I can barely stand the pain.

"Miranda! Miranda!"

"One at a time," Dr. Green says. "Please. We need some order."

"Dr. Green! How long have you known about this?"

"Ladies and gentlemen. Please!"

A young man, in charge of the press conference, tries to establish some kind of order. At the table with Ariel and me are Dr. Green, Mother and Father.

"Now, Dr. Green, if you'd like to answer."

So Dr. Green goes through the sequence of events. I can hardly listen. But I remind myself — I always thought this would be my worst nightmare. But my worst nightmare was actually that moment when I thought Ariel was dead. Of course, I feel terrible about Eve. Terrible. But she was doomed and would have died anyway. And at least he didn't tell her what he was doing. He told her he was operating on her to save her. So she went peacefully, not in fear, but in hope. If I'd spent that night sleeping instead of looking for her, Ariel would have died too. The police told us that Dr. Mullen had arranged for two bodies to go to the crematorium the next morning. All evidence of Eve and Ariel would have been completely erased, except for the DNA he would keep in his lab in Belize.

Every once in a while Ariel teases me, pretending to be Eve. But I can tell the difference. First of all, just to be sure, while we waited for Mother and Father to pick us up at the hospital, I gave her a quiz.

"When did Mother and Father leave for their trip?"

"Last Friday."

"Where did they go?"

"Europe."

"What's the name of your best friend?"

"Jill."

"What's the favourite thing of mine you always steal?"

"Your purple sweater."

"What else?"

"Your purple skirt."

"What else?"

"Your pink shoes."

Only Ariel would know that!

When my parents took us home, I told them everything. Dad held my hand. "You won't go through this alone," he said.

"I know." And then I let him hug me. I even let Mother hug me. And then, miracles of miracles, they both hugged Ariel!

And Mother said, "We're lucky to have another wonderful daughter. This won't be easy. But we're a family. And we're going to act like one. We almost lost both of you this week. And if that should happen — well, we have no substitutes for you. And there won't be any," she assured me. "Never again. Nobody could ever replace you."

And you know, they've behaved just like real parents over the last week. Protecting me and Ariel however they can. Dad did make a pretty good book deal. But I'm okay with that.

I haven't been back to school yet. Don't know if I'll be able to. That'll be the hard part. I mean, what must Mrs. Dean have thought when she realized I was telling the truth! Heart attack time, no doubt.

"Miranda!" Dad is tapping my hand.

"Yes?"

"There's a question for you."

"How does it *feel* to be a clone?"

Hah. The big question. I think how best to answer. "I don't know. Confusing, I guess. I don't know what's me, what's Jessica, what's genetically engineered. I'm not just a clone, remember. I'm also enhanced."

"So how do you tell?" the reporter asks.

"I don't," I reply. "I wonder, but I guess everyone wonders, don't they? You know, was I born with that? Did I get that stubborn streak from Gramma or my artistic ability from Mom or Dad? I guess we're all programmed to a certain extent, right? But then, well, I guess we all have our own soul. And I must have one too, right? And that means I have free will. Eve was my clone. She made some very bad choices."

I think about the most shocking thing Ariel told me when she was feeling better. Dr.

Mullen had given Eve the job of kidnapping Ariel, so he could get rid of both her and Eve — although of course Eve didn't know about what he had planned for her. But Eve herself had thought of the idea of getting me in trouble, discrediting me, and making my life miserable. Why? We'll never know, I guess. But maybe because she was jealous of me and my friends and my parents and my happiness, and she did it out of pure spite. Dr. Mullen approved, of course, because it had the advantage of making anything I said unbelievable, but it was Eve's idea!

"Does that scare you?"

"What?" My mind had wandered again.

"Does it scare you that Eve made such bad choices?"

"No!" I reply. "It gives me hope that I really can choose for myself."

"But Eve was sick!" Another reporter calls out. "Could that happen to you?"

Dr. Green interrupts. "It could happen to you, sir. None of us knows what the future will hold."

Suddenly Ariel stands up. "I'd like to say something." The room becomes quiet.

"I just want to say Miranda is a good sister.

You shouldn't be so concerned about her being a clone — you're forgetting that she saved my life. She's a hero. Well, she's my hero."

She sits down.

I reach over and give her a big hug.

"Actually Ariel saved my life," I say. "So she's my hero."

I see Emma and Ben at the back of the room. Emma gives me a thumbs up. I grin. I thought I'd never smile again once the news got out. But hey, I'm tough. I can take it.

And Dr. Green is right. Who knows what the future will hold?

CAROL MATAS is the author of many books for children and young adults, in a variety of genres. She is best known for her historical novels, including *Footsteps in the Snow* in the Dear Canada series, *The War Within*, *After the War*, *Lisa*, and *Daniel's Story*. *The Dark Clone* is the last book in the trilogy that began with the best-selling contemporary thrillers *Cloning Miranda* and *The Second Clone*. Carol has received many honours for her work, including the Silver Birch Award, the Red Maple Award, the Jewish Book Prize and two nominations for the Governor General's Award. She lives in Winnipeg, Manitoba.